Maple Moon

Connie Brummel Crook
Scott Cameron

Fitzhenry & Whiteside

To my grandchildren
Sarah and Kathryn Beranger, and Alex and Ryan and Jordan Floyd
— C.B.C.

To the Native spirit, Wenebojo.
— S.C.

I would like to thank Mr. C. Frank Cowie, Chief of
Hiawatha First Nation; Aileen Irons of Curve Lake Reserve
for helping with the language and culture of the Missisaugas,
and Bob and Marie Steele of Peterborough for their very helpful
suggestions. Thanks also to Kathryn Cole of Stoddart Kids for her
support and encouragement. — C.B.C.
Thanks to Dr. Mima Kapches, head of the department of Anthropology
at the Royal Ontario Museum for lending her expertise. — S.C.

Text copyright © 1997 by Connie Brummel Crook
Illustrations copyright © 1997 by Scott Cameron
Book design: Kathryn Cole

Published in Canada in 1997 by Stoddart Kids.
Reprinted in paperback by Fitzhenry & Whiteside in 2005.

Published in Canada by Fitzhenry & Whiteside,
195 Allstate Parkway,
Markham, Ontario L3R 4T8

Published in the United States by Fitzhenry & Whiteside,
311 Washington Street,
Brighton, Massachusetts 02135

www.fitzhenry.ca   godwit@fitzhenry.ca

Canadian Cataloguing in Publication Data
Crook, Connie Brummel
Maple moon

ISBN 0-7737-3017-6 (hardcover)
ISBN 0-7737-6098-9 (pbk.)

1. Missisauga Indians – Juvenile Fiction.
I. Cameron, Scott (Scott R.). II. Title.

PS8555.R6113M36 1997   jC813'.54   C96-932236-4
PZ7.C76Ma 1997

Fitzhenry & Whiteside acknowledges with thanks the Canada Council for the Arts, and the Ontario Arts Council for their support of our publishing
program. We acknowledge the financial support of the Government of Canada through the Canada Book Fund (CBF) for our publishing activities.

 Canada Council Conseil des Arts
for the Arts   du Canada

 ONTARIO ARTS COUNCIL
CONSEIL DES ARTS DE L'ONTARIO
an Ontario government agency
un organisme du gouvernement de l'Ontario

Printed in Canada by Copywell

A long time ago, in the heart of the great forest, in a clearing filled with wigwams, there lived a young Missisauga boy. The clearing was on the south side of a gently sloping hill. At the bottom of the hill was a small lake, called Rice Lake, because of the wild rice that grew there.

All kinds of trees grew in the forest — maple, willow, spruce, balsam, and birch — and gave shelter from the northwest winds. In summer, those winds brought rain. In winter, they brought snow.

The year the boy turned eight, the snows came early. The children of the clearing loved it. They ran between the wigwams kicking up drifts and throwing snowballs. The boy watched and wished that he could join their circle. But he was different.

When he was a baby, he had injured his left leg and it hadn't healed properly. Now he always limped and never joined in the games. Sometimes one mean boy, Fast as Lightning, would taunt, "Limping Leg, come and play!"

But the boy only stood in his hooded raccoon cloak, wishing he could.

Only some of the children called the boy Limping Leg. Everyone else used the name his mother had given him — Rides the Wind. She called him that because of the sled his father had made him. With Nimoosh pulling, the boy could move faster than any of the other children. Nimoosh was a big, strong, shaggy dog that was half timber wolf. Rides the Wind loved him and he loved the winter.

But this winter was different. The drifts were so high that Nimoosh could not get through them. The ice had frozen thick on Rice Lake and fishing was impossible. Again and again, the hunters came home with no meat to feed their people. The women gave out only small amounts of wild rice and dried berries, for their supply was almost gone. The months passed until it was time for spring, but spring did not come.

Everyone in the clearing was very hungry.

One day deer tracks were sighted deep in the forest. While all of the hunters hurried away, the women and old folks built a fire, hoping to roast a great buck before nightfall. The children were sure their fathers would return with enough food for a big feast. They danced happily around the roaring flames while their elders waited and chanted prayers to the Great Creator.

Rides the Wind could not dance with the children. Even though one old woman invited him to sit beside her, he stood outside the circle, watching with Nimoosh. Then, not wanting the others to see his sad face, Rides the Wind limped slowly through the deep snow and into the woods.

Nimoosh tried to follow, but Rides the Wind wanted to be alone and sent the big dog home.

Rides the Wind struggled as far as he could until he reached a large, old maple tree. "Ninautik!" he whispered, for that was the name of all maple trees. "I'm going to rest with you for a moment." As the boy leaned against the tree's sturdy trunk, he heard faint singing drifting toward him from the camp.

Then there was a noise overhead. He looked up and saw a reddish-brown squirrel scampering along a branch. Rides the Wind stayed completely still, moving only his eyes as he watched.

The squirrel ran halfway along the limb, stopped, sat on its haunches, and held its paws under its chin. Then it looked down and saw Rides the Wind. Immediately, it bounded along the branch, glancing back at the boy as if it was trying to tell him something.

At the very end, the squirrel began clawing at the bark. When it put its head straight down on the branch, Rides the Wind thought it was going to somersault. But it didn't. Instead, it started drinking from the bare spot it had made. Still motionless, Rides the Wind watched all of this.

When the squirrel had drunk its fill, it looked again at the boy, flew back along the branch and right up the trunk to the top of the tree.

"What are you showing me, Red Squirrel?" Rides the Wind asked, but the squirrel did not answer.

Rides the Wind hopped up and down on his good leg until he managed to grasp the end of the branch. He could see a bald patch on the wood with sap oozing from it.

He took a small, sharp knife from his cloak pocket and cut into the bark a few inches from where the squirrel had scratched. Then, just like the squirrel, he drank sap from the tree. It tasted sweet! The boy stood back and saw more clear sap trickling down from the branch.

Suddenly, Rides the Wind had an idea. The sound of singing grew louder as he hurried back to camp.

Fast as Lightning called out to him as he rushed past. "Come and dance, Limping Leg!" Two other boys laughed loudly. Rides the Wind did not answer, but dived into his wigwam. The children turned away and continued their dance.

Inside the wigwam, Rides the Wind found a hatchet and two birchbark baskets. Then he stuck his head out, and when no one was watching, he limped to the edge of the clearing and returned to the woods as fast as he was able.

"Now, Ninautik," the boy said when he reached the maple, "will you give me more sweet sap?" Setting one of the birchbark containers against the trunk, he grasped the hatchet and made a cut in the tree. Since he was only eight years old and the bark was very thick, the cut came down on a slant. Sap trickled out, but it dribbled this way and that along the rough trunk. Only a bit ended up in the basket.

So Rides the Wind peeled a piece of bark from a fallen birch tree and fit it into the cut in the maple. His idea worked. All the sap dripped down into the basket.

He sat down and waited as the day became warmer and the sap ran faster. "Good," he thought to himself. "I will have lots to take back to camp. I can surprise mother with it."

Finally, as dusk settled over the land and it became chilly again, Rides the Wind picked up the heavy basket and set it aside. It was filled nearly to the top with wonderful sweet water. He placed the empty basket under the spout and lifted the full one carefully. He did not want to spill a single drop.

Above him, the squirrel chattered happily and twitched its bushy tail.

By the time Rides the Wind arrived home, a pale moon shone high in the night sky and the hunters had returned. The women were crowded around the day's kill. It was only a thin, small buck. Everyone looked sad. The singing had stopped, though the fire still burned brightly.

"Where have you been?" his mother demanded when she saw the boy standing in the shadows. She grabbed him and some of his precious water slopped over the side of the basket.

"Look!" he said. "It's sweet water from Ninautik."

"You silly boy," she scolded. "Give me that water." She threw it on top of the fresh meat she had just cut up and dropped into a clay cooking pot. "At least it will save me from having to go to the lake for ice water. I spent so much time today looking for you, I'm behind in my work."

"But, it really *is* sweet water," the boy said with a downcast face.

Then the child's father stepped forward and said firmly, "Go home now, Rides the Wind."

With only Nimoosh for company, the boy turned and limped sadly towards the wigwam. He was angry with his parents for shaming him in front of all the other children. He opened the entrance flaps and dragged himself over to his bed of cedar boughs.

All the while, the delicious sweet water bubbled and blended with the meat that simmered in the big, clay pot.

Two hours later, Rides the Wind was startled by his father's voice. "Wake up! Wake up!" His father pulled him from his bed and led him out of the wigwam. He sounded very excited, but he did not sound angry.

"What's wrong, Father?" the boy asked.

"Nothing, Rides the Wind. The elders want to ask you some questions."

The man and boy walked over to where the elders were sitting. His father took Rides the Wind into the center of the circle. The small boy was very much afraid. Were they going to punish him for spending the whole day in the woods? He was glad that his father was holding his hand.

The chief spoke. "We want to know where you found the sweet water."

Rides the Wind answered. "From Ninautik. I saw Red Squirrel sipping the water. So I drank a little too, and it was good." The boy explained how he had cut a hole in the tree's trunk and collected the sap to bring home.

"Tomorrow, we will go to see. Now, taste this." The chief scraped a bit of food out of the pot and offered it to the boy.

Rides the Wind took a bite while the chief and the elders watched. It was delicious. He had never eaten such sweet deer meat before.

As Rides the Wind walked back to the wigwam, his father smiled down at him proudly.

At sunup the next day, Rides the Wind and his father gathered with the chief and the elders. Rides the Wind was on his sled. Enough snow had melted the day before that Nimoosh could now get through the drifts.

As Rides the Wind led the elders away, the children and younger women poked their heads outside to watch. The boy's mother stood smiling beside their wigwam. Rides the Wind turned and saw Fast as Lightning. The nasty boy was mouthing the name "Limping Leg." He did not dare say the words aloud, since Rides the Wind was beside the chief.

Rides the Wind held his head up high and paid no attention. He led the group towards the maple tree at the edge of the woods.

The night had been freezing and Rides the Wind shivered in his hooded raccoon cloak. The sun had not yet warmed the earth. Father was carrying a bearskin blanket and Rides the Wind wished he could wear it.

When they entered the woods, the child pointed to the tree. He got up off his sled and limped over to it. But his father hurried on ahead and stared down into the basket. Then he looked sadly at Rides the Wind and shook his head.

The boy couldn't believe his eyes. Only a little iced sweet water was frozen in the bottom, and there was no sap running from the cut into the basket. He blinked back tears, but he knew he must not cry.

"I'm sorry," his father said to the chief. "My boy is a teller of stories."

"No!" shouted Rides the Wind. "I do not tell stories. It is true!" His father just shook his head and looked at his son sadly. Then he turned the boy around and walked him back toward the sled.

"Wait!" said the chief. "At what time yesterday did you come to this tree?"

"I stayed all day," Rides the Wind answered.

"Then *we* shall stay," the chief said. He did not smile, nor did he frown, but Rides the Wind was worried.

They all sat down on bearskin blankets at the foot of the tree and waited in silence.

When the sun came out and shone fully, little frozen puddles began to melt and rivulets of water streamed around them. His father spoke to Rides the Wind. "Did you scoop up the water from puddles like these?"

"No, Father. I took it from this tree. Look!" He pointed to Ninautik. Once again, sap was dripping off the piece of bark sticking out from the trunk. A steady trickle of sweet water fell into the birchbark basket.

The chief reached over and cupped his hands under the dripping sap. Then he tasted it and smiled. "It truly is the sweet water. We will take it from many more trees like this one." He looked up at the sturdy maple and smiled. "Thank you, Ninautik." Then he turned to the little boy. "And thank you, Rides the Wind. Because of you, we will not starve. We will boil this water into the food we found at the bottom of our pot last night. It will make all our meat taste sweet. The Great Creator did not give us a big stag, but our prayers have been answered in a much better way. Tonight we must give thanks for your discovery with a celebration. We will call it the festival of Ninautik in the time of the Maple Moon."

Then the chief smiled. "And tonight, I will give you a new name," he said. "It will be Wise Little Raven. And when you grow big, we will call you Wise Raven."

The boy looked up at his father and saw his eyes shining with pride. "Now, my son, no one will laugh at you again."